# The Gray Ghosts
of Taylor Ridge

Books by Mary Francis Shura
The Gray Ghosts of Taylor Ridge
The Riddle of Ravens' Gulch

# The Gray Ghosts of Taylor Ridge

by Mary Francis Shura

Illustrated by Michael Hampshire

SCHOLASTIC BOOK SERVICES

New York   Toronto   London   Auckland   Sydney   Tokyo

Copyright © 1978 by Mary Francis Shura. All rights reserved. This edition is published by Scholastic Book Services, a division of Scholastic Magazines, Inc., 50 West 44th Street, New York, N.Y. 10036, by arrangement with Dodd, Mead & Company.

12 11 10 9 8 7 6 5 4 3 2 1          11          8 9/7 0 1 2 3/8

Printed in the U.S.A.          11

# Contents

# 1

## The Genuine
## Army-Navy Compass

I HATE winter.

If I were an animal instead of a thirteen-year-old boy, I would choose to be a bear. I would get fat and then sleepy and at the first frost I would curl up in the warmest cave in the woods and wait for the first robin of spring, or whatever.

A lot of my friends think that getting their mittens frozen around hockey sticks or flying down hills on sleds, creating their own sub-zero wind chill factors, is great fun. Not Nathan Miller. For me the good life is the warm one, a crackling hearthfire, cocoa with lots of marshmallows, and the curtains drawn against a bleak sky.

Another thing I am not crazy about is my ten-year-old sister, Nan.

Those are the reasons why it is so ridiculous that Nan ever managed to get me out on Taylor Ridge in the coldest January ever recorded in our part of Missouri.

The only way she could have managed it was with blackmail.

So she blackmailed me.

She was sitting on the back steps waiting for me that Tuesday night when I got home from school. She was all curled up in my outgrown down jacket that Mom had let her wear on a field trip that day.

Slumped over like that, Nan looks little and helpless. Little she may be, but helpless is a laugh. That is one kid who knows how to take care of herself. She has my mom and dad so thoroughly hoodwinked that they can't even see what is happening to them. This girl is the original all-seeing eye. Seeing everything is not so bad, but she also has an all-telling mouth. Ever since she learned to talk, I have been in trouble for things I didn't even know she saw me do. There's no way you can work around Nan, you just have to stay way away from her. I have a rule that I don't talk to her unless I absolutely have to. And the whole thing out there in the chill of winter came about because I broke that rule.

Since she is too big to step over, I just waited on the walk, tapping my foot to suggest wordlessly that she move aside and let me in out of the cold. Instead she looked up at me with those all-seeing eyes, dark and scared looking.

"Nathan, you've got to help me," she said.

"Me? Help you?" I asked, not believing my ears.

From the way her mouth was twisted I could tell she was either trying to keep from crying or putting on a really professional act for me.

"I'm in big trouble," she said in a scared whisper. "I really need your help."

I don't know what made me sit down on that cold step beside her but I did. When she didn't go on, I prodded her a little.

"So what did you do?"

She couldn't even face me. She looked down and started picking at a marshmallow streak on the sleeve of the jacket.

"I went on a field trip today," she finally said.

"Okay," I nodded. She has the same science teacher that I had in the fourth grade so I know all about those field trips. Mr. Aggers is a dedicated ecologist and his field trips are the highlight of the year. The class spends a whole day studying a natural site. Mr. Aggers doesn't believe in little things like frostbite or heat stroke slowing down the march of science so he pays no attention to season when he schedules these outings. He always builds a big fire for the winter trips and the kids have instant chocolate and marshmallows along with their soil samples and sniffles. Actually, I liked those trips, getting samples and testing, being the first kid to find an amoeba under the microscope. But from the look on Nan's face, she hadn't had just exactly a jolly day.

"Okay," I prodded again. "So you went on a field trip."

"And I lost Dad's genuine Army-Navy compass," she said.

I was back on my feet in a minute. She was talking about trouble bigger than I wanted to have anything to do with.

Don't misunderstand me, our dad is no ogre. We lose his things all the time. He's always poking around the garage or the back yard trying to find a tool one of us has "borrowed." He always just shrugs and grins a little and says, "I guess when I quit missing my tools, I'll be missing you two bandits around here."

But all that understanding stops at his Army-Navy compass. Dad was in the war in Korea and he saved some sergeant's life. This compass that the sergeant gave him means a lot more to him even than the medal he got. If Nan had taken that compass off and lost it, I didn't want to be involved in any way.

"How come you had it at all?" I asked. "Don't you know what a fit Dad will throw? Where in the heck did you have it, anyway?"

My questions must have come too fast because tears began to track down her face between the dirt streaks.

"Okay, Nan," I said, sitting down again and trying to keep my voice down, too. "Where did you lose it?"

"On the field trip," she said in a tiny tight voice. "And I didn't really lose it, I just laid it down and forgot it."

I groaned. Field trip. Right away I could see that compass at the bottom of McCafferty's Pond telling the fish which way it was to the North Pole. Or being sucked into the marshes over by the river. Or even worse, lost in that tangle of brush and trees on the top of Taylor Ridge.

"So where did you go on this field trip?" I asked. I was proud of how much patience I got into my voice.

"Old Taylor Ridge," she replied. "And if you'll just go up there with me, I can walk right to the place where I put it and we'll come right back home."

"Oh, no," I said quickly. "Don't you realize how cold it is out there? And it's a mile from here to where we would have to leave the bikes. And even after that it takes forever to fight your way through the brush up that hill."

"I was out there today," she reminded me, staring at me levelly. "Please, Nathan."

"Not on your life," I said, shaking my head. "You knew better than to fool around and take that compass. You'll just have to take your punishment."

"Mom wouldn't let me go anywhere this late by myself," she went on as if she hadn't heard me. "But if you and I went together, she would know I would be safe because you're already thirteen and she doesn't know you do dumb things like take that compass when you go on hikes, or that you even took it on that long bike trip with Doug and Jamie the week before school started."

Suddenly something in my chest got colder. I stared at her for a long time, but she held her eyes open so that I had to blink first.

"That's blackmail," I told her.

She shook her head. "How can it be blackmail? I was just explaining that I never would have thought to take the compass on my trip if I hadn't seen you do it more than once."

After living with that kid for ten years, I know when I am beaten. "Okay for tomorrow night," I suggested. "It is already getting late and tomorrow might even be a warmer day."

She shook her head firmly. "The compass might be gone by then. It could even get rained on and be ruined for good. I know exactly where I put it down. We'll just go straight there and then come straight home."

As much as I resented being bullied by that kid, I could hardly blame her for trying anything she could. I could imagine too easily how desperate she felt.

"So what will I tell Mom?" I asked, admitting defeat.

"She always likes it when you go to the library to look things up," she suggested primly. "Maybe you could just say you needed to look up something and I was going along. She would probably just add the library part on herself and you wouldn't even be telling a lie."

"You have a tiny little pea-sized criminal brain," I told her bitterly, getting up off the step.

She only slid over so I could get inside the door.

That was the coldest mile I ever biked. I couldn't get it over with in a burst of icy speed because she was trailing behind on her little three-speed and I would lose her. The sky was already darkening when we got to the fence of the Taylor farm but the sun was still visible as the center of a fused brightness just over the ridge to the west of us. Down the road a little ways I could see a cabin. A frail blue wisp of smoke rose lazily through the surrounding trees. I wished I could just stop and warm some selected parts by that fire before starting my climb. But Nan was officiously locking her bike to a fence post that bore a big sign NO TRESPASSING. Down the fence a few feet was another one that read NO HUNTING ALLOWED.

"We can't just barge into a place that is posted like this," I protested.

She climbed under the fence and pulled her scarf down from over her mouth to answer.

14

"We were all out here today on that field trip and nobody minded," she said.

Then, just as if she owned the place, she started off up the narrow, dirt-packed path that leads to the top of the ridge. There was nothing for me to do but follow.

My field trip to Taylor Ridge had been in the spring. The place had looked a lot better then. As Nan and I clambered up the slopes, sometimes following the path and sometimes cutting through the brush, the whole place started looking spooky to me. It felt like danger was waiting all around us. Big rock masses, bearing the tracery of dead vines, seemed poised to roll down on us. The limbs of the trees, naked of leaves, clawed with black urgency against the fading sky.

Nan would make a great Indian scout. She moved without hesitation. I knew she was leading me right when I heard the moan of the sycamore trees that I remembered from the time before.

Those sycamores are as old as any trees in our county, Mr. Aggers said. They were planted when the original Taylor house was built up there way before the Civil War. He had pointed out that the pioneers chose such hilly sites so they could keep out a good watch for Indians. He said they must have dug a well up there, too, but all the signs of it were gone by this time.

The brightness from the sun had faded when Nan and I reached the crest of the ridge. She was excited and very sure of herself even in that half dark.

"Look there," she said. "There is an auger hole that my partner and I made. And there's another." She ran forward into the gloom. "And right over there is where they finally stopped the big fire."

"I didn't know they had a fire up here," I said, staring about at the blackened clearing that lay between us and the next grove of trees.

"It happened only a year or so ago," she explained, relentlessly moving on. "A big fire almost took this whole hill, Mr. Aggers said. He showed us where new seedlings are starting but it's too dark to see them now. And right around this bend is the old house where I left the compass."

Then she stiffened and stopped dead still. I had heard it, too, and my breath suddenly came very hard. From the cover of the trees just beyond us came an unmistakable sound of warning, the low vibrating rumble of an animal's growl.

I never saw the animal at all. I only saw the shining of its eyes at a long thin angle as if they were half closed. The eyes seemed very close to the ground as if the wolf, or whatever it was, were already crouched to spring at us.

Nan slid over against me until she was pressed tightly to my right side. Her breathing sounded shallow as if she couldn't get the air to go down into her lungs.

All sorts of wild thoughts went through my head. Maybe I could find a big branch close by and beat off the animal when it attacked. Maybe we should make a loud noise and try to scare it away. The only thing I knew we mustn't do was turn and run for fear it would start after us the moment we moved. I tightened my arm around Nan with my head spinning with choices.

I didn't have to make any decision at all. The softest, spookiest voice I ever heard spoke suddenly from the thicket where the animal crouched. The voice wavered, hanging on the wind, coming more like the moan of a sycamore tree than a human voice.

"Go back where you came from," the voice said. "Go back to your own place and time. There is nothing for you here."

When the sound ceased, I took a single step backward, pulling Nan along with me.

"Go," the voice commanded, a little louder. "Go while you still have time."

Nan startled me by suddenly wriggling free of my grasp. She started down the hill running. She shouted back at me, "Run, Nathan. Run before he uses his gun."

The word "gun" was all I needed, I guess. I turned and fled down the hill after Nan.

The moment we started to run the dog began to bark ferociously. Some trick of the wind made his barking seem first near and then terribly far, as if it were not one dog but a whole pack of them driving us down the hill toward the road.

Nan ran like a young rabbit, darting back and forth, ducking the overhanging limbs that lashed me across the head and shoulders until I had to keep my folded arms up to protect myself.

As I struggled in the dark to unlock Nan's bike, I fought for breath. "You really saw a gun?" I asked. I know what a huge imagination that kid has.

She nodded. "It had two holes in it," she said. "And he pointed it over to the side of us."

"The side of us?" I asked. "Why would he do that?"

She didn't answer my question. She only leaned against me a minute as I handed her the bike. "Oh, Nathan," she said, "I was so scared. It's going to be so hard when we come back."

"Come back!" I exploded. But she had already started down the road, her little bike wheels waggling from side to side on the rough ruts.

# 2

## Boomer and Bubba

GOING BACK to Taylor Ridge was the last thing
I ever meant to do, compass or no compass.
But after dinner that night, Nan started in on
me again.

"Just one more time," she pleaded. "We
would go right after school when there's lots of
time left in the light. We might even ask permission from whoever lives in that cabin down
on the road."

"What are you kids plotting?" Dad asked,
coming into the family room to get his pipe.
"What cabin is that?"

"The one on the road there below old Taylor Ridge," Nan said. "We had our field trip
out there today."

To my surprise, Dad grinned broadly as he
poked in his pipe with that little metal tool he
keeps in his tobacco jar.

"That's where old Boomer lives," he said. "I haven't seen him or his dog around town for a long time now."

"Is he a friend of yours or something?" Nan asked with interest.

"You might say that." Dad laughed. "Everybody likes old Boomer. He's a harmless guy, even with his habit of stretching the truth. He's a kind of local character, in a way. He has lived out there on the Taylor place ever since I can remember. He and his boy Perry used to come to the store all the time. Then they had some trouble and the boy left. After that, Boomer always had a big Weimaraner with him. But as I say, it's been a while since I've seen them."

"He's probably getting too old to make the trip," Mom commented from the door. "I never knew him to own a car."

"Nor a phone for very long," Dad added with a grin. "Remember how he said that a phone never brought him anything but bad news so he had it taken out? He said he didn't aim to pay bad news to travel any faster than it had to."

Mom smiled back at him but she looked concerned after a minute. "You really think he's out there on that big place all by himself?"

"I'm pretty sure of it," Dad said. "He never had any family until he took in Perry Saylor after the boy was orphaned. Then, after they came to a parting of the ways, he just stayed on by himself the way he had before. Except for the dog, Bubba."

"And that's been a long time," Mom mused. "Must be a year or two."

"About the time of the big fire out on the ridge," Dad said. Then he turned to Nan. "You say Mr. Aggers took your class out there? How much permanent damage did that fire do?"

"A lot of trees and brush were burned," Nan replied. "But Mr. Aggers said that the forest is starting to heal itself. I liked the place. I was asking Nathan to ride out with me after school tomorrow."

I tried to catch her eye but she was not about to glance in my direction. Dad was looking very pleased because it worries him that Nan and I aren't better friends.

"That would be fun, Nat," he told me. "That old pre–Civil War house site is one of the few left around here." With his pipe stuffed just right, he started for the door. "Great old guy, that Boomer. Famous liar."

"What kind of a way is that to talk in front of the children?" Mom protested.

"Only the truth," Dad told her. "You remember those wild tales he used to tell us, about being captured by cannibals and almost eaten on a Pacific Island during World War II? And how somebody in his family drove a wagonload of little kids through the Civil War battle lines when both sides were firing?"

"He's just a lonely old man who tells stories to keep himself in company," Mom said softly.

"Does that mean that when I am lonesome I can tell great big whoppers and it will be all right?" Nan asked in that fake innocent voice she sometimes uses.

Can you imagine my getting a laugh with a line like that? But because Nan said it, they both roared.

Dad was practically in the next room before he turned and came back. "Be sure and give old Boomer my best wishes when you see him tomorrow," he said.

I groaned inside.

"See?" Nan asked softly. "They don't care at all. And if you go this one time I promise never ever to ask you to do it again."

"Solemn promise?"

"Solemn promise," she repeated soberly, her round eyes full on my face to be more convincing. "Solemn promise, death do us part." She always says that "death do us part" bit and, even though I know it doesn't mean a thing, that night it made me nervous because of the gun and all and I wished she had some other way to firm a promise for herself.

By the time she and I reached the door of Boomer's cabin that next afternoon, I had decided that the man on the hill with the dog had to be Boomer and his Weimaraner. But it still made my flesh creep to hear that voice come from inside the cabin.

"All right," the same soft, threatening voice we had heard on the ridge called. "Who's out there?"

"Just the Miller kids," Nan piped up. "Our dad is a friend of yours."

I could hear movement inside but it took him a while to get to the door. I looked around the place, at the great old swing hung from a tree out back. That must have belonged to his boy, Perry, I thought. Actually it was pretty neat around there except for a mop and a washpan hung on nails right outside the door.

The cabin was small, but a great big stone fireplace was filling the air with sweet woodsmoke just like it had the evening before.

The funniest thing about the place was a line of metal eyebolts that had been driven into the trees between the house and the road. Somebody had strung rope through those bolts in a kind of zigzag path as if he had marked it off for a fence to go in but never gotten it done.

Then the old man opened the door and looked out at us, frowning a little. He was little and thin, even for an old man. His eyes were almost level with mine, and I'm only five foot seven but mean to grow a lot more before I am through. His hair was pale and thin so that you could see pink scalp through the strands. But his eyes were the strangest thing about him, a cloudy kind of blue to gray that was really scary looking.

"Miller, Miller," he was repeating aloud in that soft sort of ominous voice. Then he smiled suddenly and stepped back to motion us in. "Why, of course. You must belong to that young Miller who owns the hardware store in town."

"That's right," I said, following Nan into the

cabin and watching the dog beside him all the time. The dog wasn't exactly threatening but he didn't look very friendly to me, either. "Dad sends his greetings. Says he hasn't seen you in town for a long time."

The old man ran his hand lightly along the dog's back as he spoke. "Bubba and I don't make the trip like we used to. What can I do for you kids?"

Because I was afraid that Nan would launch into some big tale, I spoke up quickly. "My sister was out here on a field trip yesterday and she lost a compass. We really need to find it because—"

Nan jumped in when I hesitated. "It has sentimental value," she finished smugly.

"Sentimental value," he repeated softly, staring past me in an eerie way. "I know how that is, right enough. My paw gave me a pocketknife when I was just a tad. I carried that knife for years, into the jaws of death in the Pacific and right out again. It was my pocket piece. Then one day, right in these woods, I laid it down in a tree and lost it. I must have looked for that knife for two years or more. My boy—er—somebody else—finally found it. The tree had grown clear around that knife so that all that was left was a tiny golden ring hanging out of the bark."

"How did you ever get it out?" Nan asked.

"I didn't even try," he admitted. "I just left it there. I figger I added one more treasure to the treasures of Taylor Ridge."

Nan glanced at me with a puzzled look but I just shrugged. This was probably one more of Boomer's tales that Dad told about.

"It's because of the treasures that this place can't rest," he went on. "That's what the gray ghosts are after, the ones that come chinking around here by night. Treasure even draws the dead, you know, on phantom horses that stamp and whinny like real beasts. But if you try to get near one, he'll silver off into the fog or the trees and all that is left is the whinny still hanging in the wind."

Nan and I just waited, not knowing what to do. Then Boomer sort of caught himself and tightened his voice as he stroked the dog's back. "What am I doing, keeping you two here? You need to go get that compass and get off this ridge before dark comes. It just ain't safe for living things when those gray things come after nightfall."

He moved us toward the door, keeping his

hand on Bubba as he walked. "Just do your looking while it's still light," he warned. "And tell your paw he seems to be raising a pretty fair set of pups."

The path that led from Boomer's to the ridge was a lot easier to follow than the trail we had taken the day before. In the full light of afternoon, the place didn't even seem spooky. It was sad and dead looking, with dead leaves piled against the trees. Among the piles of leaves were still a few with some color from fall, but most of them were just part of a dark-ish mass that had rotted in the winter rains. Once in a while we heard rustling in the thick-ets and one old gray squirrel was really curious about us. He would race from tree to tree and then spiral around it to inspect us as we passed.

But the wind rose as we neared the top of the ridge and the howl of the sycamores was even louder than on the day before. As usual Nan ran ahead. We were almost to the crest when she suddenly slowed down and let me catch up with her.

"Do you feel like we are the only ones up here?" she asked in a hushed whisper.

"I know we're not the only ones," I said

crossly. It was bad enough for Boomer to let his imagination run away and talk about horses that faded into mist and gray things that chinked at night. Nan didn't have to start dreaming up anything else to be spooked about. "There are squirrels and rabbits and wood rats. We're just lucky we haven't run into a skunk, now that I think of it."

She shook her head without smiling and glanced back into the trees we had passed. "I mean a real person," she said seriously. "Somebody watching us, maybe even following."

"We know who the spook of this ridge is," I reminded her. "You must have seen that double-barreled shotgun standing there inside the door of that cabin."

But she wasn't listening. Instead she stared down at something beside the path.

"Quit dawdling, Nan," I told her almost sharply. "This wind is going through me clear to the bone. Remember," I added, "this is the last chance you have up here. I am not going to come again."

She followed along but she wasn't really listening. Instead she walked steadily toward the site of the old Taylor house with a funny wooden step, a frown puckering her forehead.

I looked back to see what she had seen that made her so thoughtful. From the corner of my eye I thought I caught a glimpse of something moving in the thicket just behind me. Then it was gone. I picked up speed and stamped along the ridge. My gosh, between her and that old man, now even I was seeing things that melted into the trees.

# 3

## The 1858 Gold Eagle

WITH THE WIND pressing steadily against us, Nan and I moved slowly along the top of the ridge, past the dark area where the fire had been and the grove where Bubba and Boomer had scared us so much the night before. Beyond those trees the path led slightly below the top of the ridge so that the rise of earth on our left cut off the driving wind a little.

The path fell lower and lower until the slope above us was the height of a man, a tangled uneven wall matted with old vines of wild grape and stunted young trees which clung desperately among the masses of dead leaves.

When Nan disappeared around the bend ahead of me, I knew from her cry of pleasure that she had reached the old house site.

The place looked just about as I remembered it, a level clearing with the outlines of

31

rooms still evidenced by piles of trash that had blown against the remains of the foundation walls. A tall heap of fire-blackened stones showed where the hearth had been.

Instead of just running across the clearing, Nan walked carefully along the line where the outside wall had been. Then she stopped to look back at me. "This was the door," she said, her eyes gleaming at me over her shoulder. "And the parlor is right over there." She motioned airily with her hand as if she were a model or something.

As she walked through that imaginary door, she was suddenly holding both mittened hands out at her sides as if she were wearing a hoopskirted dress instead of my old marshmallow-stained jacket. A gust of wind from the hill cut through me, sending a shiver clear into my boots. Being cold always makes me angry and for her to start playacting while my bones were turning to icicles made me shout at her.

"Stop the act," I yelled. "Get the compass so we can leave this polar icecap."

Her face fell at my tone and her hands went swiftly into the pockets of the jacket. Without looking at me she walked dejectedly toward the fireplace stones. Something about the angle of her head made me feel guilty. After all, that kid is only ten (which is pretty young for the trouble she can cause), and I had to admit it is natural for a ten-year-old like that to playact.

And I didn't mean just girls, either. Standing there inside that room whose walls had suddenly risen again in her imagination, I knew she really felt herself become a child of that other century. In all honesty I used to do the same sort of thing when Dad took me to the battlefield at Lexington, Missouri. While Dad walked along the broad Missouri River, staring out across the water to the marshes beyond, I played soldier among the trenches. The distant sounds of traffic turned to artillery barrages in my ears, and a cold clutch of fear would flatten me against the grass as I felt the waves of enemy soldiers fighting their way toward my battalion—which, of course, was always cut off from supply and being led by a captain or something because our commander had been shot from his great white horse at the beginning of the battle.

"After you find the compass, you can show me how the house was arranged and all," I called to her, as a sort of apology.

When she didn't reply I walked on over to the pile of fireplace stones she was climbing awkwardly, clinging to the rocks with her mittened hands as she went.

"Be careful up there," I warned her. "How come you put it so high?"

She didn't meet my eyes and her voice sounded embarrassed. "I pretended I was hiding it from the enemy soldiers," she explained. "Like people always hide treasure when armies are fighting all around."

With my arms clasped around my shoulders, I danced a little to warm my legs while she clambered to the top. Then I saw her lean over to fish around in a crevice between some stones. It seemed to me that it took her a long time. When she finally turned and looked down at me she had a strange, confused expression on her face.

"What's the matter?" I asked.

She only frowned and turned away to dig frantically in that same hole again.

"It's not here," she said finally. "It's just plain not here any more."

"Then what's that stuff in your hand?" I asked.

"Just stuff," she said defeatedly. "Stuff that wasn't even here before." As she spoke she started throwing things angrily to the ground. "Some old metal and sticks and leaves." Her voice grew crosser with every word. "Where's the compass, Nathan? I know I left it here. I am positively positive this is the really honest place I left it."

"You could have made a mistake," I told her. "There are lots of rock piles around here. Maybe it's that one over there."

"This is the right place," she said stubbornly, still perched on top of the rock pile and staring down at me. "I was a teenager and very pretty. My mother was dead and my father was off shooting in the war when the enemy came riding up that hill." She pointed so convincingly at the ridge behind me that I barely stopped myself from looking around to see. "They were beating on their horses with whips and shouting terrible yells."

Then suddenly Nan was acting it out. "I climbed up here and hid the family treasures in a loose stone in the fireplace where they would never think to look . . ."

"And what was your partner in the science

project doing all this time you were doing an instant rerun on the war?" I asked sarcastically.

She tossed her head in that funny, defiant way that makes me want to laugh. "If you must know, he was my great admirer and he was squatting in that window right behind you and loading and reloading his musket to hold back the intruders."

I didn't want her to see my grin so I leaned over and picked up the dark metal thing she had thrown near my feet. It was round and heavy and coated with black. I rubbed it absently between my fingers and tried to talk her down off her perch.

"Well, that war is over." I told her. "And if you don't want to start a new one with Dad you better start thinking of some other place you might have left the compass."

"It was here, Nathan," she wailed, her anger having cooled to tears. "This is the right place and it's gone."

"Even you can make mistakes," I coaxed her. "Try one more time. After you and your civil war partner played this little game what happened?"

"We heard the whistle for everyone to go

back to the bonfire," she said, sniffling. "So I just ran."

"Then you are sure this is the only pile of rocks you could have left it on?"

She nodded. "It's the only one I even climbed on—the fireplace one."

"Maybe Boomer himself was prowling around up here and found it," I suggested. "After all, we know he came up here with Bubba that night after your class left."

"Surely you're kidding!"

"Not so," I said. "He wouldn't know whose it was or anything, so why shouldn't he pick it up?"

She was climbing back down the rocks and stopped to stare at me again. "How could a blind man find a little compass like that hidden up in a dark place in the rocks?"

I stared at her dumbly. Blind man. What kind of a weird head did that kid have, anyway? Boomer had strange-looking eyes all right, but lots of old people have a kind of misty look in their eyes like that.

Before I could get my head together to answer her, the air was suddenly alive with sound. Like a gray streak, Bubba raced past us through the clearing, barking from the great strength of his massive lungs. Then he topped the ridge and plunged into the woods on the other side of the crest. His barking was so ferocious that I started after him, curious about what had set him off on that wild chase. But I stopped at the sound of Boomer's frantic voice behind me.

"Bubba," the old man was calling wildly. "They are friends. They are friends."

Looking back, I saw Boomer bracing himself against one of the sycamore trees at the edge of the clearing. He held onto the trunk with one hand as he shouted in the direction of Bubba's barking. His face was dead white with fear. "Bubba, come back," he wailed.

Realizing why he was so scared, I ran to him as fast as I could. "Bubba chased some animal over the hill," I told him. "Nan and I are all right." I could still hear, from the other side of the ridge, the crashing of Bubba's pursuit through the trees.

"He didn't go for you," the old man said with relief. "One minute he was with me and then he was gone . . . I was afraid . . ."

Nan went over to him and slipped her hand into his as naturally as if he had been Dad. "We're fine," she said softly. "Bubba must

have seen someone . . . something else . . . over the top of that hill."

Boomer's voice was trembling with relief. "Thank God, thank God," he said, leaning heavily against the tree. "I thought he had gone for you for sure. Yet it wasn't like him not to know his friends."

The barking had ceased and within minutes Bubba dragged himself back over the top of the hill. He was panting heavily and his tail hung dejectedly as if he had disgraced himself by letting his quarry get away. I watched the dog come up beside Boomer and slide his back in under the hand that Nan had taken.

Blind. Nan had said that Boomer was blind. That would explain his pointing the gun to one side of us that first time. It would explain why he hadn't recognized us when we went to his door to ask permission to look for the compass. It explained so many puzzles that I hadn't even tried to solve.

But now he was happy. With his hand tender along Bubba's back, he asked if we had found the compass.

"No, sir," Nan said unhappily.

"Well, maybe you just looked in the wrong places," Boomer said. "Since the house is gone, everything looks about the same up here."

"That's what I've been telling her," I said.

"A fellow can easy mix up one place with another," the old man went on. "Like the way I lost my penknife that time. I could have sworn I remembered which tree I laid it in." His voice trailed off a little and he glanced convincingly at the sky. "Darkening soon," he warned. "Can't have you on this hill when the night comes in with those gray ghosts and all."

Nan hung back, tears brightening her eyes. "Nathan," she pleaded.

I shook my head. "We've done all we can," I told her. "If that is the right rock pile, we have just done all we can."

She bit her lip and turned to run down the path in front of us. I knew she was crying and I felt awful, but what could I do? I'd done everything I knew to help her and she wasn't any farther along than she had been in the beginning. I would have been sorrier for her if she had even tried to find the compass on any other rockpile, but she was so pigheaded certain. All we had gotten for our pains was getting half frozen to death and a little piece of black metal.

Remembering, I pulled the metal circle from my pocket where I had been absently rubbing it with my wet mitten. I stopped dead in my tracks. The silly thing had changed color. There was a dull black stain on my mitten but the metal thing had taken on a burnished yellowish tone. I turned it over and stared at it a couple of times before I could even get my voice to work.

"Look here," I said to Boomer, forgetting about his blindness. "Nan found a coin up there. We thought it was just an old piece of metal but it's a gold coin . . . a ten-dollar gold piece."

The old man stopped dead still, his hand gripping Bubba's back as he stared at me, open mouthed.

"Is there a date on it?" he asked quietly.

I rubbed the coin hard a few more times and then I could make it out. "Right under the head of Liberty," I told him, "it says 1858 as plain as you please."

Nan had paid no attention to me. She was still plodding dejectedly down the hill ahead of us, her mind full of the loss of Dad's compass. But she turned and stared up at us with a puzzled frown when Boomer let out a great shout.

"It's still here," he yelled, his face blazing with sudden color. When he reached out I handed him the coin and he fingered it reverently. "I was right," he said solemnly. "This gold eagle proves I was right. The old Taylor treasure is still hidden here after all these years."

# 4

## Old Tales and New Terrors

THE EXCITEMENT of our finding the old coin set Boomer to chattering like a little kid. He even forgot to keep up his pretenses of being able to see. Instead, he clung to Bubba's back as the dog cannily led him where the ground was smoothest and the pathway free of jutting branches.

It was only when we reached the flat yard that surrounded his cabin that Boomer stopped for breath. Then he looked around with a sudden frown of concern. "Where's that little girl?" he asked nervously. "We didn't leave Nan up there on the hill, did we?"

"I'm right over here," Nan replied from the front step where she had sat down to wait for us.

"Are you all right?" Boomer asked. "Not hurt or nothing?"

"No, sir," Nan replied dolefully as Boomer, with Bubba close against him, opened the door of the cabin and motioned for us to go in before him. Through the open door came the rich scent of beef and onion and spices in a rush of steamy air. My stomach churned with hunger even though I always think I can't stand vegetable beef soup.

"Well, you two sit down and warm yourselves a spell before you start home. I wish I had some sweet or another to offer. I know how younguns like sweets. But Bubba and I don't keep such truck around since . . ." His voice trailed off with a note of irritation.

"I'd like to warm up a little," I agreed, peeling off my mittens to spread my hands in front of the banked fire. "What about you, Nan?"

"Whatever you say," she replied listlessly.

"You sure you're all right, child?" Boomer asked again, obviously concerned at her tone.

"I think Nan is just down in the dumps because she can't find that compass," I explained.

"Well, child," he said soothingly, "maybe it

45

will turn up again, another time, just like my penknife did. If it only has sentimental value, losing it can't take that much away from you."

"But it wasn't mine," Nan said miserably. "It belonged to my dad. He'd going to be mad as anything at me."

"Your dad," Boomer said thoughtfully. Once inside the house he had moved with sure steps through the room, running his fingers along the edges of furniture until he located his own chair. Bubba flopped on the braided rug at his feet and laid his fine lean head between his paws.

Then, as if he had thought it over carefully, he shook his head. "Your dad never seemed the kind of man who'd be unreasonable," Boomer said.

"It was his most cherished thing in the whole world," Nan said unhappily, letting herself down to sit cross-legged in front of the fire. "I don't think he will ever forgive me."

Boomer leaned over and groped in a basket under the table by his chair. One by one he selected three apples and laid them on his lap. Then he began to polish one between his hands in light, buffing strokes, not even looking at it but staring toward the fireplace with a frown. "He'll forgive you all right," he assured Nan after a minute. "Even if he gets powerful mad and says a lot of things he will wish he could pull back later, he'll forgive you. Dads are like that."

The fire crackled suddenly and a log dropped and shattered into a scarlet honeycomb of heat. I thought about Boomer's foster son, Perry, and wondered if they had parted like that, in anger with a lot of words said that Boomer wished he could pull back later. The room was too still with Nan and Boomer both lost in their thoughts.

"Can I put another log on for you, Boomer?" I asked, as much to break the silence as anything else.

"Say, that would be helpful," he said, rousing a little. "And while you're at it, hand this apple to Nan, there. I'll shiny one up for you, too. No point in your starving on the way home."

When Nan thanked him for the apple she added sulkily, "I don't ever want to go home again, not without Dad's compass. How did that silly coin get put in where I had the compass, anyway."

"You seem mighty all-fired sure you looked

47

in the right place," Boomer told her.

"I am positive," Nan said stubbornly. "I know exactly where I put it."

"And what did you find when you went back?" Boomer asked.

"Just that coin that Nathan called an eagle and a handful of brush and twigs."

Boomer shook his head in a confused way. "I can't believe that treasure hunters would leave that valuable old coin and take something new like a compass."

"That wasn't a new compass," Nan corrected him. "It came clear from the Korean War."

"Korean War!" Boomer said. Then he began to chuckle and finally to laugh so hard that he had to wipe away a tear that started down the deep wrinkles of his cheek. Bubba rose and glanced questioningly at his master before turning to curl again on his rug. "Why, that Korean War was like yesterday. Do you know how long ago that treasure was buried on Taylor Ridge? And how it came to be hidden away like that?"

"Not really," I replied. I hadn't meant to eat the apple he had handed me until later, but

Nan's looked so good that I took a big crisp bite.

"I thought maybe the people who lived there were afraid of the soldiers," Nan said, "and they hid their valuables away to keep them from being stolen."

Boomer nodded. "Right on the truth there. This was a hard part of the country during the Civil War. This state had people from both sides of the war and the battle lines sometimes were drawn between one farm and another; between one brother and another, even. There was a lot of bad blood in these parts during that war and it made for a lot of bad battles.

"This place here, the Taylor Ridge Farm," he went on, "was a good example of that. Moses Taylor owned this place and he believed with the North. Right down the road, there by where the gasoline station is between here and town, lived a family named Rupert, and they were just as strong for the Confederacy.

"When they started calling up men to fight for the Union, Moses Taylor was among the first to go, even though it meant leaving this

49

place and his wife Emmaline and three little younguns not big enough to care for themselves, even."

"Wasn't she afraid?" Nan asked, her apple forgotten as she stared up at Boomer.

"I reckon she was," Boomer nodded. "But she did what she had to do and tended the farm and minded her babies for almost a year before the tide of war got close to this county. The Union soldiers, knowing her husband was with their army, were good to her. They slept in the meadow sometimes and used water from her well for themselves and their horses, but she and the little ones were safe. But then the Union got driven back and the other army came through.

"One of the Rupert men led the raiding party. They took all the food on the place and butchered her milk cow for meat and ate the chickens. What they couldn't carry they burned out, a barn full of hay and all the wagons but one old relic that was out in the field where they didn't see it."

"But they didn't hurt Emmaline or the children?" Nan asked breathlessly.

"They didn't get a chance to," Boomer said with a short laugh. "Whenever she saw horses coming, she bundled up her children and her treasures and hightailed it to the woods. She had a cave up there to hide them and when the soldiers had gone she would bring her little ones back home. That last time, when she came home to empty cupboards and the smoking ashes of her barn, she faced up to the real danger she was in."

"With all those babies," Nan said, her eyes shining with sympathy. "Poor Emmaline!"

Boomer chuckled. "You wouldn't think 'Poor Emmaline' if you knew that redheaded girl. She looked at that ruin of her home and stamped her little foot in anger. With winter coming on and no food, she knew her children would starve if she didn't do something. With the guns of battle just north of her, she set to work. She traded china dishes and a woolen mantle to a neighbor for a broken-down mule named Dick. When the neighbor had him hitched to that old farm wagon, she bundled the children in all the clothes they owned and bedded them down in the back.

"She knew she would be stopped and searched. Everyone had heard stories of the woman Union spy Pauline Cushman, how she dressed like a man and played tricks on the rebels. So with the children packed in the wagon, she hid all the treasures that she and Moses owned, their store of gold coins and the flatware she had gotten from her family. Not even the children saw where she hid that hoard.

"Then she set off north as spunky as you please, coaxing that old mule along and singing to her babes so they wouldn't be scared by the rumble of the fighting up ahead."

I glanced at Nan, who stared back at me with a nod. I knew she was feeling the same way I was. Dad had mentioned this same story as one of Boomer's "whoppers" but, as Boomer talked, I could just see that redheaded girl and hear her frail singing against the sound of distant guns.

"She did get through all right, didn't she?" Nan asked, nodding her head as if that would help make the story end right.

"After just one close call," Boomer said. "By the time it was nearing evening, they were close to the line of battle. The baby was cutting teeth and was feverish, the way babies get. The nearer they came to the sounds of fighting the more scared Emmaline got and the more the children fretted and fussed. She had no food to give them so when she saw a little stream she stopped the wagon and took her younguns over for a drink and a splash of water on their faces. She was kneeling there with her feverish baby in her arms when she heard hoofbeats coming along the road.

"Later she said the idea came to her like a candle being lit inside her head. She grabbed a handful of ripe elderberries and dabbed that baby with red spots everyplace you could see his skin.

"Then the horsemen were there and the officer leading them shouted to her, 'Stand forth and be recognized.'

"With her baby in her arms she stepped forth from the woods, but before she could even speak one of the men called out, 'It's that redheaded Taylor woman. She's a Yankee's wife.'

"With the guns of his men leveled on her, the officer dismounted and swaggered toward her in an insolent way. 'Yankee wife,' he sneered. 'More like Yankee spy!' Then he told her how she and the children would be taken prisoner and the mule and the wagon would be 'commandeered.'

"He underestimated Emmaline. She knew

he wanted to hear her cry and plead for mercy for herself and her children. Instead she smothered her anger in a defeated tone and spoke very craftily to him.

" 'Do what you will with us, sir,' she said in a heavy voice. 'The mule is broken down and the wagon rotted. As for my children and me, we have not long to live, anyway.'

"Wondering at her words, the officer drew nearer. When he saw the baby's fevered face and the dark spots on his flushed skin, he leaped back with a cry.

" 'Good God,' he shouted. 'These people have the pox.'

" 'The pox,' his men screamed, scrambling away as if the wagon itself were about to explode.

"At that moment the baby began to wail weakly and the other younguns, flushed with heat from their heavy clothes and hungry besides, joined in with their wailing.

"The officer, from a careful distance, told Emmaline to pack her babes back into the wagon post haste. She was to drive north, he said briskly. One of his men would ride ahead to insure passage into Northern territory. 'Spread your death among your own kind,' he said triumphantly, obviously pleased with his cleverness."

"I like that Emmaline," Nan said with satisfaction.

"Most everybody did, I reckon," Boomer said thoughtfully. "They say there was a great sadness when she died of diptheria the year the war ended, before she even saw her husband again. But she never told anyone where the family treasure was hidden."

"And you think it is still here?" I asked.

"Lots of folks have looked and some folks even think that the soldiers found it right away, but I know better. They've dug up everything, the fireplace, the old storage cellar, every place a girl like that might think of hiding things, but they haven't found it yet."

"What makes you so sure?" Nan asked.

Boomer chuckled. "Here, Nathan, reach up there on that shelf and hand me down that blue-and-white teapot with the picture of an onion on it."

After he fished in the pot for a minute, Boomer pulled out a coin and handed it to me. "See there?" he asked triumphantly.

"This is a double eagle," I said. "A real double-eagle, twenty-dollar gold piece."

"That's right, son," Boomer said. "I found it on the floor of the woodshed where I had left a pile of shiny new fence staples."

Nan and I waited, confused, before Boomer went on. The tone in his voice when he spoke was almost impatient. "Don't you see?" he asked. "It's wood rats. Somewhere around here is a colony of wood rats. They know where the treasure is and they trade pieces of it for what they want, like fence staples, or a compass."

"Like pack rats out West?" I asked.

Boomer nodded soberly. "Just the same, they've been around here for years. Why, I could tell you stories . . ." Then his voice suddenly stilled. Bubba, who had rested quietly all that time at his feet, turned to stare toward the window, whining softly. "It's them," Boomer said in that defeated, hollow voice. "Didn't you hear that chinking?"

I hadn't heard anything and Nan just looked confused but Boomer hastened us home, telling us to go swiftly past the road beneath Taylor Ridge.

We started out fast enough but after only a few yards Nan stopped her bike and cocked her head toward the hill. I pulled up beside her. Beyond the ridge some streaks of sunset color still trailed across the sky, but on our side of the ridge the darkness flowed in among the trees and down the hill toward Boomer's cabin. In the crisp chill I heard the far barking of a coyote, the cry of a bird in flight, and a strange, repetitive sound like metal striking gently against stone.

"Chinking," Nan said quietly. "The gray ghosts are chinking, just like Boomer said."

"You're nuts," I said angrily, ashamed of the tightening in my chest and the strange way my hair seemed to move by itself under my woolen hat. But the sound stayed in my mind all the way home and I kept remembering that uneasy sense I had felt when Nan and I first went up on the ridge.

# 5

## Unchangeable Nan

I NEEDED TO TALK to Nan before we got home. I had to beat it into her head that it was time to give up and tell Dad the truth and take her punishment (or ours if it worked out that way). I tried pedaling right beside her to talk to her but she just kept shaking her head and pretending she didn't understand what I was shouting at her.

"You got to give it up," I yelled. "You got to tell Dad what you did."

She just kept her eyes straight ahead and pedaled like she was in an Olympic race or something. What a bullheaded kid!

I let her wheel her bike into the garage first and then I had her trapped. "Okay, Nan," I said sternly, standing between her and the garage door so she couldn't dart away from me. "Face facts. The compass is gone and lost as thoroughly as that treasure of Emmaline's is. It's all over at Taylor Ridge, okay?"

"I'll decide when to give up," she said sullenly. "And I'm not quite ready."

Something in her look warned me. "I've gone out there for the very last final time," I told her.

"Nobody asked you to go," she said hotly, her jaw stuck up at me with that stubborn tilt. "There could be other ways."

Other ways. I wondered. To be quite honest, I had already given a lot of thought to what Boomer said about the wood rats, where they make their nests, and all. If I knew enough about them, maybe I could find the nest myself. But it wouldn't be like Nan to think about researching. She had something else in her weird head. Had those all-seeing eyes noticed something up on Taylor Ridge that I had missed? Boomer's story was so similar to the playacting that Nan had done up at the house that it was spooky. I've never thought much of Nan, but the way she grasped the whole idea of that place out there, the way she had realized Boomer's blindness even while he tried to conceal it, had sort of impressed me. And the chinking—the chinking had been for real.

"Boomer's mad," I said angrily after a minute. "And I'm beginning to think his craziness is catching."

She looked at me as if she felt sorry for me. "You could be right," she said in that quiet tone. "His blindness may be catching, too. He's not the only one that gets an idea stuck in his head and won't let it go until thunder. Or can't even see a horse in front of his face."

I was pondering her words when she dropped her mitten on the garage floor. She bent to pick it up and, quick as a shot, darted under my arm and flew up the drive to the house.

When I got inside she was sitting on the floor pulling off her boots with that innocent look that fools everyone but me. When I glared at her, she made a face behind Mom's back too quick for anyone but me to see.

It took me clear to bedtime to get really warmed up. I sat all bundled in an afghan trying to keep my mind on my homework. But how could I be expected to work math problems when all I could think about was wood rats?

That had to be the way to find the treasure. All the logical places had been searched.

Boomer said so himself. The fireplace stones, around the foundation, even the root cellar (wherever that was) had surely been gone over stone by stone. The only way left was to find the wood rats' burrow and take it from there.

I checked out our books at home without much luck. There was a lot about Norway rats and roof rats, the kinds that had originally come into the country from other places and carry disease and damage things. It seemed funny that there was so little about wood rats, or trade rats, or pack rats, which are really native here. I did learn that they have bushy tails more like squirrels than rats but there was nothing about their nesting pattern.

That was all right, I decided. I had two study periods that next day. I would just research those rats and slip out to the ridge without Nan knowing about it. I'd told her I would never go again with her, but I hadn't said I wouldn't find that compass and Boomer's treasure by myself. I'd show her who was blind and set in his ways like Boomer!

When I settled down in the library I had a pretty good time. I learned a lot of stuff I didn't know. I've always been fascinated by stories about lemmings, how they all gather and rush off the cliffs to die in the sea. I didn't know that wood rats were the same family as lemmings and that we have lots of lemmings in American forests. I read about a lot of different kinds of wood rats but couldn't find one that might live in our part of Missouri. I was beginning to think that Boomer's talk about the pack rats was one of his "whoppers."

The librarian glanced at the books I returned and grinned at me. "Going all out on the rodents, Nathan? Got a problem at your house?"

"Not really." I laughed. "I was trying to find out if we have a wood rat around here. You know—" I guess I was showing off a little, "the ones that are native, with the bushy tails."

She puckered her forehead thoughtfully and leafed through one of the books I had laid down. "I know the rat you mean. I used to see them on my dad's farm. They don't look all that ratty, with the dark streaks on their heads and backs. I think they are called Illinois wood rats—really cute and not scared of people like those nasty Norway rats are."

"Would you hold that book for me until my

next study period?" I asked, getting excited again.

She nodded, still reading in the book. "*Neotoma,*" she murmured softly.

"Thanks a lot," I said with a grin. "Neotoma to you, too." She smiled and put the book on the reserve shelf for me.

When I got back I found out she was right. The rat was *Neotoma* and was called the Illinois rat even though its range includes parts of Missouri and Arkansas as well. Any doubt I had about one of those rats being able to carry off the compass was gone when I read that they measure from fifteen to over sixteen inches long, full grown. By the time I left for home I knew more about rats than I needed to know. My head was stuffed with great stories of stuff they have carried off, rivets from blacksmith shops, buckles and coins, and pieces of silverware right out of women's cupboards.

But the most important thing I had learned was that when wood rats are close to people they tend to make their nests in low hidden places, in among crevices in rock piles, in old holes, and even in the attics of abandoned buildings. From what I knew of Taylor Ridge, I could think of a dozen places to look without even trying.

The house was quiet when I got home so I fixed some hot cocoa and got down a plate of cookies. I dreaded that cold trip out there and figured I might as well stoke the old furnace before getting it out into the blast. I had finished one cup of cocoa and was pouring the second when the phone rang.

"You and Nan all right?" Mom asked. "I meant to be back by now but Dad needs me here at the store and I can't get away."

"I'm fine," I told her. "But Nan's not here."

"That's strange," Mom said. "Where do you suppose she is?"

I restrained the smart answer that came to mind and told her I didn't have any idea.

"You don't suppose she went out to visit that old Boomer again, do you?" Mom's voice was mildly concerned. "That's all she has talked about these past few days."

"It's possible," I agreed, a funny little discomfort starting in my chest.

Mom paused and then decided aloud. "I can't imagine she would go out there by herself. She would have waited and asked you to go along, wouldn't she, Nathan?"

"Maybe, maybe not," I replied, remembering how plain I had made it to Nan that I was not going to help her any more with her problem. It was just like her to grab a chance like this and go off up there on her own and get into trouble.

"I might just take a swing out there and check," I suggested.

Mom's reaction flowed warmth over the phone wire. "Oh, that would be so good of you, Nathan. I'd really appreciate it."

"Not a big deal," I said, telling her good-bye.

While I hassled my jacket back on I decided that Mom must have guessed right for sure. Nan had definitely seen something out there at Taylor Ridge that she hadn't told me. And that was strange. Before now I thought that little monster always told everything she knew. Maybe she just blabbed when she was sure it would get me in trouble.

I couldn't believe that the temperature had dropped that much during just two cups of cocoa. I went back inside and put on an extra sweater under my jacket and made another hot cup of cocoa with two marshmallows to reward myself for being a good guy and freezing myself for a sister I couldn't stand anyway.

Then I launched myself for the *third time* into the icy, blasting wind between home and Taylor Ridge. I was mad.

# 6

## Darkness on the Ridge

THE LIGHTS were already lit in Boomer's cabin when I glimpsed it from the road. When I knocked at the door, the old man appeared so quickly that it was almost as if he had seen me coming.

But his face fell at my greeting. Clearly he had not been expecting me.

"Nathan," he said with surprise. "I thought you were Nan and Bubba come back from the ridge."

I was still in the doorway, shifting from one foot to the other to warm my chilled toes. An unreasoning anger started in me. I had been right about Nan, and now that silly kid was up there in the growing dusk on that hill. I controlled the tone of my voice carefully. "Then she went up there with Bubba?"

He nodded, staring past me into the fading

light outside the door. "I didn't want that little child alone up there so I insisted she take the dog along. She was so dead set on looking for that compass again." His voice grew plaintive. "It does seem a long time they've been gone."

Then he cast a sly sideways glance toward me and added, "I would have gone to find them myself, except that my old wound from the war was giving me fits. When it's cold like this I can't get around so good."

Why don't you just admit that you can't see and quit making up stories? I asked him silently. Something about the way he fooled himself filled me with annoyance. But it was his problem, I reminded myself. Nan was my problem, as little as I wanted her to be.

"That's all right," I said. "I'll go up and bring the two of them back."

He was obviously relieved and stood in the cold of the doorway as I started off. Then he called after me, "Remind Nan about them gray ghosts that come with night. Get her back down before the dark settles."

I didn't answer because I figured he wouldn't hear anyway. I knew it was getting colder by the minute and the wind battered and whined in the woods about me. I took the

68

straightest path to the crest of the ridge. I started shouting for Nan as soon as I reached the burnt-out place. I would call and stop to listen for a reply and then press on into the wind.

The first few times I got no answer I figured I was still too far away. Then I decided that the wind sweeping off the ridge was carrying the sound of my voice away from where they were. Even if Nan was too stubborn to answer, I knew that Bubba would respond to a voice by barking.

Then I was on the top of the ridge and the sun was almost gone and the eerie silence was broken only by the howl of the wind and the moaning from the sycamore trees. I was cold inside and out and angry at myself for the fear that turned in me like a twisting thread.

"All right, Nan," I shouted angrily. "This isn't funny any more. Come on out." When no answer came, I whistled and clapped my hands and shouted. "Hey, Bubba, come on. Here's a boy."

The silence that fell after my shouting was heavy with foreboding. Where could I even look for them? I wondered desperately. The house was gone and beyond me stretched only the woods and the ridge with trees marching along its crest. They couldn't be hurt, not both of them, not hurt enough that neither of them could answer.

There wasn't even a sign that a dog and a kid had been there. I searched the ground, thinking maybe I could see the tread of Nan's boots or a dog track from Bubba. Nothing. I started walking ever wider circles around the site of the old Taylor house, calling and calling and watching the ground for some sign.

I was maybe twenty-five feet away from the house when I stopped in amazement. There were marks of horses' hoofs, lots of deep, U-shaped marks as if the horses had stamped heavily on the frozen earth in anger or attack.

You're making that up, I told myself fiercely. What good would it do to scare myself to death with wild ideas? I just kept walking and shouting until I was farther along the ridge than I had ever been before. The light was dim and I was just scared enough of the wind-stirred shadows that moved in the trees that I wasn't watching my step. My foot hit something that gave on the forest floor. There was a funny tearing sound and I stumbled down onto one knee. At first I thought I had just turned my ankle but, when I tried to stand up, my foot was caught. I pulled and tugged hard before I got it loose. When I did, I heard again that funny sound like old wood rending. I was leaning over rubbing my twisted ankle when I heard a strange, muffled sound. It was as if a dog was barking deep inside the earth.

"Bubba," I shouted excitedly. "Bubba, keep barking!"

The sound came again, dimmer and then stronger, according to the gusts of wind.

My foot still hurt and the old rotted board I had broken had torn an ugly, jagged hole in my boot that I knew Mom would get pretty hot about, but none of that mattered now. I limped along carefully, all bent over like an old man to hear better. I shouted and listened and shouted and listened. The sound seemed to come from the other side of the ridge and I started up that path. Then suddenly, Bubba's voice seemed very close although still muffled, and I heard Nan shouting something I couldn't understand.

"Bubba! Nan!" I cried, staring at the side of the ridge. "Where are you?"

"The door," Nan shouted. "There's a door." Then her voice was drowned out by Bubba's excited barking.

A door? I stared at the edge of the hill. There was only that rise there above the path, tangled with vines and dead leaves. I scraped at the hill and found only another layer of old dead humus underneath that.

They were still shouting and I was still searching the area and getting absolutely nowhere at all. Yet they were there, inside that stupid hill somewhere. Mad at myself, I kicked the side of the hill hard with my good foot, feeling the earth give a little at my blow. I kicked again and again, and suddenly I heard a dull, hollow sound and the earth didn't give at all. I was kicking something solid. The door.

Nan had called it a door but I would have said "trapdoor." It was a bunch of flat boards fastened together with crosspieces of wood. The whole thing was dirty and stained and crusted with dead leaves and vines so that it looked like the dirt bank it was set into. I could hear Nan and Bubba behind it, but I couldn't figure out how to open it.

"There's a stick," Nan shouted. "You push up with a big stick. Up."

Sure enough, a stout pointed stick lay on the ground near the door. I shrugged as I reached for it.

"Up," Nan kept shouting from inside. "Up."

Without even being able to see the bottom of the door, I rammed the stick into the dirt where I thought it must end and pried up. I didn't lean much weight on it before the door flew up and slid back into the hill. Bubba leaped out of the darkness in a whirlwind of gratitude. For about a minute there he had a hundred tongues and all of them were flapping me wetly in the face. Nan crawled out behind him, grubby and crying with relief.

She straightened up and stared at me. "I found the old root cellar," she said, still a little breathless. "I sure am glad you came."

"How did you manage to lock yourselves in there?" I asked, relieved and angry and curious all at once. But even before she replied I had guessed the answer. The minute I let go of the stick the trapdoor dropped quickly, concealing the hole in the hillside as completely as before.

"I propped the door up with that stick to go in and look around," she explained. "Bubba heard something and lunged toward the door.

When he knocked the stick down, we were both trapped in there."

Bubba was gone. After running a few great, loping circles of gratitude, he had headed straight down the hill for the cabin.

"So what would you have done if I hadn't come looking for you?" I asked acidly, watching her brush dirt and leaves off her jacket and slacks.

"I guess we would have had to wait there until the gray ghosts came back for their things."

I stared at her. What a kid! Here she was, rescued from practically being buried alive, and all she could think about was that silly ghost story of Boomer's. I shook my head with disgust and strode ahead, leaving her to run down the path behind me, still babbling.

"But you don't understand, Nathan," she protested, jumping every third or fourth step to try to keep up. "There are gray ghosts all right, but they aren't real ghosts. They wear something like a rubber blanket with a hood and armholes. And they keep their chinking tools in a green canvas bag."

"Sure, sure," I said, trying to go faster than

she could keep up. "That old root cellar hasn't been used for over a hundred years but the guy still comes back from the dead to use the tools he kept there."

"Nathan, listen to me," she pleaded. But I was at Boomer's front door. He waited there, a frail silhouette against the light from inside, a shadow of a man with a massive dog under his right hand.

"They sure had me worried, that pair," Boomer admitted as I spoke.

"The dark slipped up on them," I said, feeling only a little guilty at my half truth. "We better get on home before the folks start worrying, too."

All the way home Nan kept on about the tools and the gray thing. I just pedaled ahead and refused to listen to her, the way she had done to me the day before. Finally, when we stopped in our own driveway, she lost her temper.

"All right, Mr. Know-It-All," she said crossly. "You want to explain *this* to me?"

She was thrusting something in my face, a piece of wrinkled, colored paper that smelled like mildew. When I saw what it was, I snorted with disgust.

"So it's the same *Courier* we get at our house every day," I told her.

"Look at it," she insisted, waggling it in my face.

I pressed out the rumpled paper. It was a torn-out article about Mr. Agger's fourth-grade class planning a field trip to Taylor Ridge. The date was above the article in the corner. The paper's date was the Monday just past, the day before Nan's class had gone out and she had lost Dad's compass.

"You really found this in the root cellar?" I asked.

She nodded soberly. "Along with those gray things and tools that are shiny, not all rusted like old ones. I figure that whoever is chinking up there at night saved this to remind himself that he should stay away that day."

I was thinking hard and I guess she thought I still didn't believe her. "And there are horses that come, Nathan. Maybe it's only one horse, but I saw the manure that first day so there is a horse, just like Boomer says."

"I know, I know," I muttered numbly and went on inside.

# 7

## Proof Positive

MOM NEVER comes to school to pick us up. For one thing, Dad usually takes our only car to the store with him. For another thing, our folks don't believe in hauling kids around. They consider it "coddling" in a little town like ours. Nan's school is two blocks east of the house and mine is about three blocks in the other direction, so it would be silly to start up an engine and waste energy for such a little distance to drive.

Sometimes I fool around with my friends a little at school before starting home. That Friday afternoon I ran into Steve Davidson by my locker and we stood there gabbing a while. I had been so wrapped up in Nan's problem and had spent so much time running back and forth to Taylor Ridge that I felt out of touch with everything. Steve and I had been standing there maybe fifteen minutes when Steve frowned past me and asked, "Hey, isn't that your little sister?"

I turned to see Nan coming down the hall with that funny, stiff look kids get when they are in a big, unfamiliar building. When she saw me, she broke into a run.

After a quick, timid glance at Steve, she explained.

"Mom is waiting out front for you, Nathan. She sent me in to make you hurry."

"What's up?" I asked.

"Boomer," she said tersely, glancing swiftly at Steve as if she were not sure she should talk in front of anyone else.

"Boomer?" I repeated in surprise. "What's the matter with Boomer?"

"Mom doesn't know," Nan said, still a little out of breath from her dash down the hall. "But he sent a message by the postman that he needed you and me to come out and help him."

"Hey, that sounds mysterious enough," Steve said with a curious excitement in his face. "You don't suppose it's something about his treasure?"

I must have stared at him because he

laughed. "Heck, everybody knows about Boomer's old Civil War treasure. Boomer's been looking for that hoard ever since my dad was a little kid."

"Mom says to hurry," Nan prodded, obviously not pleased at Steve's interest. "It already started to snow."

I groaned and pulled my jacket out of my locker and told Steve good-bye. Snow. That was all we really needed to finish off a miserable week, another icy trip to Taylor Ridge with snow piled on like frosting.

The front steps of the school were slippery. I danced for balance, following Nan down to the car. The ground wasn't even white yet, but it was that fine, sugary kind of snow that freezes on everything it touches. Mom was all huddled up behind the wheel with the car heater going full blast.

"What's this about Boomer?" I asked, crawling into the front seat beside her.

She shrugged. "Nan must have told you all I know," she said, shifting gears and easing the car carefully onto the street. "Boomer apparently waited for the postman and asked him to give a message to your dad at the store. All he said was that he needed help and could you kids come out this evening."

"Here's your snack," Nan said from the back seat. "I already ate mine."

She handed me a piece of pineapple upside-down cake with the cherry gone from the middle of the pineapple. I looked at Nan and she shrugged. "Okay," she said, "so I ate your cherry, too."

Mom giggled as she saw me trying to separate the sticky cake from the soggy napkin under it. "I could have managed that better on waxed paper," she admitted, "but when I cut it I didn't think about your having to eat it in the car."

The cake was still a little warm and tasted delicious. I was so busy enjoying it that I didn't realize for a few minutes that Mom had driven right past our house and was turning toward the road to Taylor Ridge.

"Hey," I told her. "This is a lot of trouble for you, driving us out to Boomer's and all."

"Not too much," she said, peering intently through the snow that seemed to fall the thickest right against her windshield. "Dad and I didn't want you two stranded out there if this snow really started in earnest."

One thing about riding, that trip was a lot

shorter. I was still licking my fingers when Mom stopped in the road in front of Boomer's cabin.

I had never seen Boomer so upset. Small circles of bright red shone high on his cheek-bones and his eyes, usually so dull and lifeless, glittered with moisture. He only nodded at Mom and started talking real fast to Nan and me about Bubba. He said he had let Bubba out for a run a little bit before lunch time like he always did. "But he never came back," Boomer finished in a hard tone as if he were saying something unbelievable.

"He always comes back," Boomer added after a minute. "Something had to happen to keep him from coming back. He always comes back. This just ain't right."

"How do you think that Nan and Nathan can help?" Mom asked reasonably enough.

"Maybe he got into a trap or something up there," Boomer explained. "If a stranger came, Bubba wouldn't even let him come near. He knows his friends, Bubba does. I thought that the tads here wouldn't mind going up on the ridge to look for him. Something got him," he said firmly. "He'd have come back here to me if he could."

Then he ducked his head so he wouldn't be meeting Mom's eyes. "Nathan here knows about my war injury, how I can't walk so good when the weather turns bad. Otherwise I would have gone myself."

"The weather sure turned bad enough," Nan commented. "That snow is really coming down."

"Snow?" Boomer said with amazement. I almost laughed at the dumbfounded look on Mom's face. Boomer had opened the door for us and stood waiting while we walked across the solid snow cover of his front yard. Nan explained the old man's blindness to Mom swiftly by pointing to her own eyes and shaking her head. Mom nodded slowly and recovered her wits.

"Don't worry about this pair." Her tone was louder and heartier than usual. "They're wrapped up for any kind of weather. Is there any special place they should go to look?"

"He usually prowls around the old house site," Boomer said. "There's a lot of little varmints that live up there and he likes to scratch around for them. Do you suppose somebody could have set traps up there and me not seen them?"

Mom laid her hand on his arm reassuringly. "Don't start worrying yet," she said. "Nathan and Nan will go up and look around this minute. I'll wait here with you and they'll be back in no time."

As Nan and I shouldered our way up the slope against the blowing snow I grumbled a little. "I wish I was as sure as Mom that we'd find Bubba right away." The snow prickled on my cheeks and nose like tiny needles. It gathered on my eyelashes and melted into an icy stream around my eyes. The hole I had torn in my left boot on that old rotten piece of wood was letting moisture in. The third toe from the left was slowly turning scarlet and getting ready to freeze—I could just see it in there, stiffening for its death. Winter!

Nan didn't even answer me. She was too busy marching along with her mouth wide and her tongue sticking out to catch as many snowflakes as possible.

"Why would anyone put a trap up here anyway?" I grumbled to myself. "There's no game up here to speak of, just squirrels and some raccoons and rabbits."

"And wood rats," Nan added unexpectedly.

"I think that whoever keeps his tools in that root cellar has knocked Bubba out or locked him up or something so Bubba wouldn't keep him from his searching."

That girl and her imagination. I just snorted at her.

"Or that horse could have kicked him and left him lying there bleeding to death, all red on the white snow."

"Shut up," I shouted, even though that's one of the million things I am not supposed to say to Nan. "You just save your breath for climbing and quit making up scary stuff."

But in spite of myself, I picked up speed and a funny lump came in my throat at the thought of Bubba lying helpless with the snow falling on his fine long body and great gray eyes.

We started calling as soon as we got to the house site. It was like the day before when I was looking for Nan but the silence was different. It seemed as if the snow had taken all the sound on the hill and wrapped it inside itself. From only a few feet away, Nan's voice came weak and muffled as if she were yelling through a soft sack of something.

Nan was always ahead, as usual. She kept

right on going when I reached the crest of the hill and stopped to shout and listen.

"Stop crashing around," I called to her crossly. "I couldn't even hear Bubba barking with all that noise you're making."

"I want to look in that root cellar where we got caught yesterday," she called back. "Maybe he got himself locked in there again."

"How could he do that?" I argued, grudgingly following. "The door had to be pried up for him to get in. It shut down tight after you two got out yesterday."

I might have been the wind moaning in the sycamores for all the attention she paid me. She moved steadily along the ridge to the place where the ground rose high above the path.

Then she paused and turned to stare at me. "Nathan," she said with soft delight in her voice. "Listen."

Bubba was whining, whining from inside the earth just as he had the evening before. At the sound of Nan's voice, he gave a few sharp, desperate barks. It was then that I heard the other sound coming from somewhere off in the woods. It didn't sound like an animal at all, it was more like a man's voice in pain—no words, just a long moan and then silence.

Nan's eyes were as round as agates. "Who is that?" she asked in a terrified whisper.

I shook my head. In that silence the sound came again, a low moan of misery, muffled like the bark of the dog.

"Maybe we should have a big rock ready when we open up the root cellar door," she suggested. "It might be some really bad person trapped in there with Bubba and only pretending to be weak and hurting."

It didn't even sound to me that the moaning was coming from the same place but I was in no shape to argue any points. I looked around and got a rock, one big enough to stun a man with but not too big for me to hold in one hand. Then Nan handed me the stick and I started prying at the bottom of that trapdoor.

I had lifted the door only about halfway when Bubba, flat on his belly, whined out into the snow, dirty and trembling. Nan caught his big head in her arms and hugged him tight. To my astonishment, big tears were pouring down her face and she was angling her tongue to catch them as they passed her mouth. "Oh, Bubba," she said softly over and over. "Oh, Bubba, Bubba. I thought you were dead—dead and trapped and bleeding."

"Let him go," I suggested quietly after a minute, still holding the trapdoor half open. "He'll go right off home to Boomer and the old man will know he's all right."

"Okay," she agreed, her arms still around the dog's neck. "But while you've got that thing open, I want to prove to you that I wasn't just making stuff up."

I pushed the trapdoor the rest of the way up and peered in. "You think I'm a cat or something to see in that dark?"

That was when she let Bubba go and fished in the pocket of her jacket. She pulled out the flashlight Dad keeps in back of the driver's seat in the car. "I brought this along just in case."

I had to laugh. There is simply no way to win against that girl. I took the flashlight and grinned at her, "You sure are easy to hate, you know that, don't you?"

"I don't mean to be," she said in a funny, wistful voice, but she grinned a little so I felt better.

Bubba had left us and I could hear his wild barking as I aimed the beam of light into the root cellar. I figured he was just celebrating his freedom and I didn't pay any attention to his clamor.

Down on my knees in that snow, I flashed the light around the inside of the cellar and then I did it again. There was rubble everywhere, that matted leaf and twig rubble that clutters all the forest floor. There were some rotten old shelves falling away from the walls and what looked like an old broken crock with a big number glazed on the side.

Behind me Nan was hopping up and down with triumph.

"See?" she gloated. "Didn't I tell you? See what I mean?"

I didn't answer at all. I just backed off and handed the flashlight to her. "You take it," I said. "Show me the shiny tools and the gray ghost costume and all that stuff."

She squatted there a long minute and then she kind of crumpled. "No," she whispered softly. "I can't have made it up, Nathan." Her voice turned to a wail. "It was all there, Nathan, it really was."

I was getting ready to have my turn to gloat right then but Bubba interrupted it. He was still with us and he came suddenly to my side, barking loudly at me, almost desperately.

"I thought you'd be at the house by now," I told him, patting his head. "Now come on, boy. Go home!"

At my words he ran a little way away and began to bark again furiously. Then he came back, whining and barking by turn as if he were trying to tell me something, at the same time unhappy that I was too stupid to understand.

"He wants us to follow him," Nan said thoughtfully. "Like those dogs do on television. He's trying to lead us."

"Oh, sure," I said. "But he's not even going in the direction of the house."

Bubba had run away again. He stood poised on his slender legs a few feet away, staring at us pleadingly. In the quiet moment between his whines, I heard that other sound again, that noise like a human being groaning in pain.

Nan was glued against me like a lichen as we listened together. The silence covered the ridge like the falling snow. Not even a twig cracked anywhere under the piling snow. Into that breathless, waiting silence Bubba cried softly and ran off into the woods, looking back at us every few steps.

# 8

## A Cry for Help

THE DECISION was made silently. Nan and I neither spoke nor exchanged a glance. We both knew that we had to follow Bubba to the source of that anguished cry. Neither one of us wanted to go and neither of us, if challenged, would have failed to admit that we were terrified. Moving as one, we started along the path that Bubba had taken, a path leading into the snow-laden trees whose branches intertwined in a tangle of spectral white.

The snow had changed as snows usually do. The flakes had grown larger and more substantial. They fell more thickly all the time. Even without wind, the drifts had managed to pile against stones and bushes and cling to the north sides of the trees, turning them into ghostly pillars. We could see maybe two or three feet ahead but no more because of the steady layers of falling snow.

The only darkness in that place was the pattern of dog tracks where Bubba had raced back and forth pleading with us. With Nan's hand tight in mine, we followed Bubba, scarcely breathing because we were listening so hard for that painful, terrifying moan to sound again.

When we neared the place where I had torn my boot on the rotten board, Bubba grew frantic. He kept racing forward a few steps, whining piteously, and then charging back at us.

Nan was still beside me when I felt the earth give a little under my right foot. "Wait a minute," I warned her. "There's something strange here."

She obeyed silently, standing perfectly still and staring at me fixedly as her eyelashes whitened from the falling snowflakes.

Shining the flashlight before me, I inched forward. Then I saw that Bubba was circling a dark, uneven hole in the ground. About that darkness were snow-covered splinters of broken wood.

"The well," Nan cried in a tone of discovery. "Mr. Aggers said there had to be a well up here somewhere."

Because I had no idea how wide the mouth of the well would be, I lay down flat and scooted forward until I reached the edge of the dark hole. Once there, I steadied myself on the spongy wood and sent the beam of the flashlight down into the darkness of the well.

The light cast spooky shadows down the narrow, rock-lined sides before it struck something pale and tangled looking. With snow falling all about me, it was hard for me to make out what I was seeing. Then the voice came again. It seemed as near as my own hand, a hollow, pained cry: "Help. Help me."

"Help," I said aloud stupidly. Then I almost shouted at Nan. "Help. Nan, I need help."

"What can I do?" she asked shrilly, staying back as I had requested but dancing with helpless indecision.

"Not you, honey," I said more gently. "I need help from down there. The sheriff, maybe, somebody with ropes." I was startled to hear myself call her a special name like that but I couldn't stop to figure out what made me do it. I had to have someone come who could

bring up that man while he still had breath for those feeble cries.

"You run down the hill," I decided aloud, trying to keep my voice calm. "Try to get Bubba to go with you. Tell Boomer and Mom that a man is trapped in a well up here and to get help *fast.*"

She was gone at my last word and Bubba, willing to pass his vigil to me, disappeared with her into the whiteness of the woods.

I kept looking down at the tangled hair and the mass of gray so far below me in the well. As much as I hated the sound of his pain, I wanted him to cry out again, to reassure me that we had not come too late to save him. What if he died down there? What if Nan and I had not responded to Bubba's appeal soon enough?

When the man in the well gave a small moan of wordless anguish, a leap of hope warmed my chest and I called down to him, "Help is coming. Just hang on. Help is coming."

There was no reply.

That endless time that I spent waiting by the well was almost unreal. I am the Nathan Miller who hates winter and can't stand being cold and, as a matter of honesty, isn't that crazy about his sister Nan, either. But during that time, something between a half hour and an hour, maybe, I lay on my stomach on the frozen ground holding the light on the man in the well.

In no time at all Nan's and Bubba's footprints were gone and I became only another of the white mounds that marked the earth between the shrouded trees. As I waited, the light left the sky and there was only the glow of the falling snow to brighten the air. In time the snow itself seemed to be the only source of light, a vague, restless brilliance that fell steadily, burying me among the trees.

As much to remind myself of my own life as to reassure the intruder in the well, I called down to him once in a while.

"Just a little longer," I would plead. "Hang on."

Afraid that I would exhaust its batteries, I only turned on the flashlight once in a while to check that the man had not moved or slipped farther down into the shaft.

But I was never conscious of the cold. I didn't even feel cold one minute of that whole time. The panic I felt at the man's predicament made me forget myself and any discomfort I might have had. As for Nan, I leaned on her in my mind as if she were an old, strong person and not a little ten-year-old. I found I was reminding myself of what a little Indian scout she was, being able to find her way in the dead of dark (or the white of endless snow) with that all-seeing vision of hers. I felt grateful for her stubbornness at finishing things she started when any sensible person would have given up. I even told myself that her crazy imagination would help her get her part of the job done because she would be imagining all sorts of wild things that would happen if she failed.

Because the man could die. I filled my head with every kind of restless thought to keep from admitting to myself that the man down there could die. He might have already died even, and in a strange way it would be my fault.

After all, I was the one who had broken the wooden seal on that well and not gone back to check or warn anyone. People had been walking over that boarded-up hole for a hundred years with safety, but once I put my big awkward boot through it, it had trapped a man

. . . maybe even become a death trap.

I shone the flashlight down again and begged the man to cry out or something. It had been too long since any sound had come from the well, and a heaviness of grief made me hurt behind my throat. My words were interrupted by a new sound, the snarling racket of a four-wheeled vehicle of some kind, roaring up the hill. At the sound a sudden rush of tears flooded my face, feeling like boiling water on my numbed cheeks. How wild it was. The tears were pouring out like anything and I wasn't even crying. "They're coming," I shouted hysterically down into the well. "They're coming. Help is here."

The sheriff was out of the Jeep and on his stomach beside me before I could even catch my breath. "Rope," he shouted over his shoulder, "and bring that lantern over here." Then he turned to me. "Any sign of life down there?"

I shook my head. "Not for a long time," I admitted. "I kept talking but he hasn't made any noise lately."

"You down there," the sheriff shouted, while his leather-gloved hands worked with a stout rope. "Can you hear me?"

The sheriff's booming voice echoed hollowly back from the mouth of the well, and he shook his head.

Frowning at the well, the sheriff measured its diameter with his eyes. "There's no chance that I could get down there," he said thoughtfully. "Not even with my coat off. And if he can't cooperate . . ." His voice trailed off and he studied me. "Would you be game to go down after him, Nathan?" he asked.

I nodded, unable to speak around the hard lump that had already settled in my throat.

"This is the way it will work, son," he said quietly. "You'll have to go down headfirst so you can work ropes around him. There won't be much air and no light at all. You'll have to get a loop of rope about each of his arms."

He stopped and looked at me carefully. "You don't have to do this, Nathan. I'll understand just fine if you don't want to be let down in there."

I knew that if the knot in my throat got any bigger I wouldn't be able to breathe, much less talk, but I somehow croaked out that I wanted to do it.

"If you get into any trouble, just tug on the rope hard and we'll pull you right out. Hear?"

he asked. When I nodded, he added, "One more thing, you'll never make it in that heavy jacket. It's too bulky."

Until I turned to hand my jacket to one of the sheriff's men behind me, I didn't realize that Nan had come back with them. She was scrunched up against the side of the Jeep with those big eyes wide with terror. Very purposefully, I made an exaggerated wink at her and twisted a grin that I didn't really feel. She tightened her shoulders and grinned back at me, so we didn't need to say any words at all.

The ropes hurt on my shoulders with the weight bearing down on them, but the odor of the well was much worse. It was cold down there and slimy, and it smelled like time gone bad with a thick mustiness that went all the way through my nose and up into my brain.

In that tight space I could hear my own heartbeat, fast and hard. I braced my hands against the slimy, rough stones as the men let me down just a little bit at a time. Then my hands touched something soft and stringy. My fingers caught in a mass of tangled hair. As I grabbed the hair, I felt it draw away from me as if the man had shifted. I gasped with fear. Practically holding my breath, I slid the first loop of rope down the side of the man's head, along his arm, and finally over his hand, so that when the rope was pulled up, his shoulder would rest in that loop.

When I finally worked the second loop inside the man's clothes to secure his other arm, I realized that a dull, uneven thumping vibrated against my hand. He was alive. In spite of his seeming lifelessness, the man's heart was still beating.

I jerked wildly to signal the sheriff to pull me up. My head spun from hanging those long minutes upside down and I was sick at my stomach from the foul air, but the man still lived.

# 9

## The Silenced Ghost

THE MINUTE that the sheriff pulled me free of the mouth of the well, something strange happened. I went to pieces. I trembled all over and unless I clamped them tight, my teeth banged against each other. My legs seemed to have melted so that I staggered against the deputy who was holding my jacket out to me.

"Get him up there by the heater," the sheriff called. "And bundle him up tight."

I wanted to protest being treated like a kid but the deputy just nudged me up into the seat of the Jeep beside Nan. It wasn't the best place to watch the rescue from because the snow fell like a veil in the headlights, but it felt good to have Nan pressed against me silent and wide-eyed.

The man must have fallen down a whole lot easier than he came up. The sheriff and his men worked slowly for a long time, inching him up along the rough wall of the well. Finally they tugged him up high enough so that one of the men was able to reach down and seize him under the arms and pull him the rest of the way. As they hauled him free and to his feet, he was like a great, soiled moth unfolding from a cocoon. Supported by the sheriff's men, he looked huge and ominous next to the snow-covered deputies and the endless, blinding whiteness of the woods.

At first he seemed to be slumping in their arms, but after only a few moments I saw his hand emerge from the poncho and grasp the sheriff's shoulder in a strangely urgent way.

"What's he saying?" Nan whispered. "What's going on?"

We couldn't hear anything except the throb of the Jeep's engine, but we could tell that the man from the well was terribly upset. His lips moved rapidly and he pushed the tangled hair back nervously as he pleaded with the sheriff. He was too bundled up to tell if he was fat or thin but he was obviously tall. Above his beard, his face looked really young and sort of handsome in a bony, hollow way. He seemed steadily more excited as he kept struggling back toward the well against the restraining arms of the sheriff and his men.

"I can't stand it," I finally admitted to Nan. "I'll go find out what's going on. Be right back."

The sheriff didn't even notice my joining them.

"You've lost your mind," he told the young man angrily. "Never mind the well, you've got to get to a doctor . . ."

"But you don't understand," the man said frantically. Then he saw me and lunged to catch my jacket in his blood-stained hand. "You, kid, you're Boomer's friend. Make this guy listen. It's there. It's down there in the well. Boomer's treasure is there in a bucket in the well! It's the only thing that kept me from falling all the way to the bottom."

I stared at him and then at the sheriff. "What does he mean?"

"God knows," the sheriff said disgustedly. "It isn't enough that we saved his life. Now he wants somebody to go back down for a bucket of something."

Boomer's treasure. A bucket partway down the well?

I slid my jacket off and tossed it down. "Let

me go see," I said. "Just let me down like before and I'll see."

The sheriff shook his head vigorously. "There's no way I am going to risk you again, Nathan." Then he paused. The young man's eyes were fixed pleadingly on his, and I said, "Please," softly before he could go on. He shrugged and turned away from us both. "Okay," he said reluctantly. "Five minutes. If it takes more than five minutes, I jerk you up and we forget the whole thing."

At his words the young man smiled broadly and then seemed to slump as if all his energy had left him. He almost staggered against the deputy standing at his side.

Going down into that well for the second trip was both better and worse at the same time. At least I went down feet first so there was some light and enough air. But I also knew that there was nothing, no hanging man, between me and the bottom of that hole which suddenly seemed so deep that it could go to the center of the world.

With the loop of rope cradling me, I tensed against the drop as they let me down, and then farther down. The light at the top grew dim and random, interrupted by the heads of people peering in. As I descended, my hands groped against the sides of the well. There was moss, soft and spongy, and the rough edges of the stones which had cut up the young man's hands. Then suddenly the rope grew slack and I knew I wasn't moving any more.

Something sticking out from the side of the well was keeping my left leg from going down any farther. I pulled my leg in tight so that I could squeeze myself past whatever was jutting out there. Then I was level with it. A solid bucket of some kind of metal had been fastened to the stones that lined the well. I was suddenly too excited even to think. I tried to tug the bucket loose but it wouldn't even jiggle.

"All right down there?" the sheriff called, his voice echoing hollowly about my head.

"I found it," I shouted back, "but it won't come loose. It has a lot of stuff in it."

After some muffled conversation at the top of the well, the sheriff called out, "Now watch it. I'm dropping a bag."

With the unzipped flight bag open against my chest, I transferred the contents of the bucket into it one handful at a time.

We used to play a game at parties when I

was little. Everyone sat in a circle blindfolded while different objects were passed around. Everyone was supposed to figure out what the objects were just from feeling them. I could tell the coins easy enough now and there were lots of them. Then there was that leaf and twig litter, which I also stuffed into the bag because there wasn't any other place to put it. Then I reached large slick things that were very cold and hard and some of them so big that they fitted into the bag with some difficulty. Some felt like platters or plates and one had a nose on it like a teakettle or something. Strange kind of treasure, I thought, wondering if Boomer was going to be disappointed by this stuff.

When there was nothing left but leaf litter and some small, hard flakes that snagged at my fingernails, I signaled on the rope to be pulled up.

The Jeep headlights made great circular rainbows in the falling snow as the sheriff hauled me to my feet. I glanced around for the man from the well. After all the fuss he had made about bringing that bucket up, I expected to see him standing there with the others. The sheriff noticed my glance as he uncoiled the rope from my shoulders.

"He used up all his fight getting you back down into that well," he explained. "He's over there waiting in the Jeep."

I had a million questions about the man and the strange, gentle way the sheriff had treated him, but this was not the time to ask them. I was aching with cold, and a terrible heaviness slowed my steps toward the Jeep.

Still clutching the canvas bag, I crawled into the back seat beside the young man. At first I thought he was asleep, the way his head had fallen back and his hands lay so quietly along his legs. But he opened his eyes about halfway and twitched a smile at me.

"Hey, thanks, kid," he said. "Thanks for everything." Then his eyes drifted shut again and he chuckled so that the wet mass of the poncho vibrated against me. "My life may not have been worth the saving, but that last trip down there will set things right for Boomer."

The sheriff had swung Nan onto the lap of one of the deputies in the front seat. "You sit up here and navigate," he told her with a grin. "Let's see if you can get us back as miraculously as you got us up here."

As the vehicle bounced and growled

through the trackless snow at Nan's direction, I kept sneaking looks at the man beside me.

Then he opened his eyes and stared back at me. "We must be almost to the cabin by now," he said contentedly.

"Then you know Boomer?" I asked.

"Know him?" he asked with astonishment. "Why, he's all the family I've got in this world."

I must have spluttered something but he went right on.

"He took me in when nobody else would have me, years ago. He was a real Dad to me, that old man, and we really had good times. Then there was the fire."

He fell silent and I couldn't stand it. "What happened about the fire?"

His voice hardened with annoyance. "Oh, he is such an old fool. He was going blind and wouldn't admit it even to himself. We had lost a calf up there on the ridge, a newborn, and he went to look for it with a lantern. He lost his footing and spilled oil from the lantern, which naturally blazed into a big fire. We barely got that fire stopped before it took the county but he'd never admit that he had started it. He swore I had been smoking up there on the ridge and that was how it began. He couldn't face his own blindness and getting old and helpless. We had a big fight and he told me to shut up or get out. I got out for good."

"Then you're Perry Saylor," I said aloud.

He sighed. "The same."

A kind of slow anger had started in me while he was telling me about the fire. How could this guy speak so tenderly of Boomer in one minute and then do what he had done? It didn't make any sense to me. "Then you're the one who has been scaring old Boomer to death all this time," I said angrily. "You're the gray ghosts that come and chink at night. With horses that fade into the light and become invisible and all that."

He frowned at me a moment, then groaned. "Then he saw and heard me? I never thought he would, not blind as he is. And he thought I was more than one? I didn't mean to scare him. I got a job over in the next county and rode over here at night and tethered my one horse in the woods while I searched for that treasure."

"And hid your tools and that poncho in the root cellar," Nan added triumphantly from the front seat.

He nodded. "Maybe I never would have found that stuff if I hadn't fallen into that sealed-up well, but I had to keep on looking if I was ever to locate that treasure."

The sheriff's voice was hard and angry from the front seat. "You thought that treasure was going to be worth more to you than to that old man?"

Perry Saylor frowned at the sheriff's back. "The treasure was *never* for me, Sheriff," he protested. "It was for Boomer. He's blind, Sheriff. If he doesn't get help he's going to kill himself wandering around out here. He wouldn't admit it even to himself, much less talk about it, because he doesn't have enough money for doctors or even help around this place. When he almost killed himself in that fire, I was scared enough to speak right out to him about what shape he was in and what he ought to do. He wouldn't listen, told me to mind my own business or clear out. Well, I figured that yelling at him wouldn't help but clearing out might. Especially if I could find that treasure of his so he could get himself fixed up or get somebody to take care of him."

As the Jeep shuddered to a stop by Boomer's cabin, the sheriff turned to Perry. "And it never occurred to you that the story about the treasure was just made up?"

"Listen here," Perry said hotly. "My old man—I mean Boomer—has a way of telling a story that makes it seem too exciting to be true. But he never tells anything but the gospel truth."

"Spoken like a true son!" The sheriff chuckled. He lifted Nan down and set her on the snowy ground to run toward Mom, who was standing in the open door beside Boomer. Bubba, with his head cocked at a curious angle, slid from under Boomer's hand and raced toward the Jeep to welcome us.

# 10

## Finder's Fee

FROM THE OPEN cabin door came a rectangle of golden light and the sharp scent of brewing coffee. Mom's face shone with relief as she caught Nan in her outstretched arms. Bubba danced about excitedly as we all piled out of the Jeep.

Only Boomer stood alone and unreassured. Walled in by his blindness, he stared bleakly from his post in the doorway, his fists balled at his sides as if to be ready for an unexpected blow. Unable to endure the wait, he called out, "Are they back? Are Nathan and Nan all right?"

Before anyone else could speak, old Nan of the all-seeing eyes and all-blabbering mouth piped up. "We found your boy Perry, Boomer," she told him swiftly. "We found him down a well."

In the moment of stunned silence that followed, I watched a grayness sift into Boomer's face. He braced his arm against the doorway as if his legs had turned limp beneath him.

"Perry?" he repeated numbly. "Perry in a well?" The anguish of his tone reminded me afresh that all Boomer's information came through his ears. He could not see Perry, soiled and exhausted, crossing the snow-covered yard with his eyes hungry on Boomer's face.

"It's me, Boomer," Perry called hastily. "I was in the well but I'm okay now."

The fear that had paled Boomer's face was swiftly replaced by relief. He stared in the direction of Perry's voice and one hand reached out searchingly. But then, with a sort of shudder, the old man turned his back on that voice, on all of us, and disappeared into his cabin.

As if he were Nan or me, Mom just ignored him. "Come on in, everybody," she called out heartily. "There's hot coffee ready." By the time we had all crowded into the little room, Boomer was settled in his usual chair, staring toward the fire. He looked very calm except for one thing. His hand rubbed Bubba's back so urgently that the dog turned to stare at his master, puzzled.

Mom busied herself handing cups of coffee to the sheriff and his men. When she brought one to Boomer, he asked quietly, "Is he still here? Is Perry still here?"

"I am," Perry answered for himself, moving closer to Boomer's chair. His tone was firm but his eyes had that half-scared look that Nan and I always get when we know we are going to get it from Dad.

"Then it was you on that hill at nights," he said heavily. "It was you up there trying to scare me with ghosts and the chinking and all. You was after the Taylor treasure. Don't you bother lying to me like you did about the fire. You come back to find the Taylor hoard, didn't you?" His voice rose steadily in anger as he spoke. He seemed to have forgotten how grief stricken he had been when he thought Perry might have been found dead in that well. Now he was angry and accusing, and so aggressive that even the sheriff shifted his weight from one foot to another with embarrassment.

But Perry stood very straight and stared back at the old man so stubbornly that you would have thought he didn't know that Boomer was blind. He looked messy to be standing there so full of dignity. His poncho was all torn and streaked with mud and stains. His hair and beard were tangled from his imprisonment. The snow melting off his head had washed uneven streaks through the dirt smudges on his face. I guess I expected him to be apologetic like I always am when Dad raises his voice to me, but I just didn't know Perry. He spoke back at Boomer in that same resentful tone that the old man had used.

"It's me right enough, Boomer, and it was the Taylor hoard that I came back to look for." He paused only a minute before adding triumphantly. "And I found it, too, if that's going to be your next question."

Boomer was all set to lash back at the young man but his face slackened with surprise. His words came out weakly.

"You found it?" he asked. "You've got the Taylor treasure?"

"Correction," Perry said firmly. "I found it but I don't have it. Your friend Nathan has it all right here in a canvas bag."

At that Perry took the bag from me and set it on the old man's knees, waiting a moment before taking his hands away until Boomer's veined hands closed over the canvas. "It's all there and all yours. I just hope it hasn't come too late for you."

Boomer twisted nervously, his hands tight around the bag. "Don't you start telling the world that something is wrong with me, you young pup," he said angrily. "We came to a parting of the ways once over that and it can happen again."

"Nobody has to run me off of anywhere," Perry said stiffly, wiping the back of his hand across his face to stop the rivulets of water still streaming from his hair. "I got what I came back for. With the money from that treasure you can do something about that sight of yours. Or at least hire somebody to take care of you out here before you kill yourself."

"Mind your business," Boomer almost shouted, his voice trembling with anger. "Who asked you to come in here and meddle with my life, to tell all these folks lies about me?"

"Oh, boy," Perry groaned softly, almost to himself. "Talk about old dogs and old tricks."

The rest of us had just stood there stunned while they fought with each other. It was Nan who broke in with her eyes wide on Perry.

"Then you just went for that treasure to fix Boomer's blind eyes?" she asked.

"I AIN'T BLIND," Boomer shouted with such force that Bubba, under his hand, leaped with surprise.

Nan stared at Boomer a moment and then went over and knelt down by him with her hand on his. "Don't be a silly, Boomer," she said reproachfully. "Everybody knows about it. That first time Nathan and I came out you could have killed us with that big gun and you didn't even know we were just kids. You can't make yourself see just by saying that you can. Why, you could have killed us and not even known it."

Boomer paled at Nan's words, and when he spoke his tone was softened.

"Not blind, Nan," he corrected her. "Maybe my vision is dimming a lot but I ain't blind. You see, child, if I was blind, they'd make me leave my home and go in town to live. I can't be blind, I just can't."

"Not blind," my mother said gently. "I'm no doctor, Boomer, but your eyes might have cataracts like my grandmother's did. After her operation she went back to reading the paper

every day, and she even lets down Nan's hems for me."

The sheriff set his coffee cup on the sink with a thump. "Well, that's all to be settled later," he said. "I was called out here to get a man out of a well and here he is safe and sound. Now I just need to know what charges to bring against him."

"Charges?" Boomer asked.

The sheriff nodded. "After all, he was trespassing on posted land. He's been disturbing your peace up there on that ridge. Then we caught him hanging in a well with the Taylor treasure tight in his scratched up hands . . . red-handed, you might say." He grinned a little at his joke, but Boomer was frowning unhappily.

"Perry?" he asked quietly. "What was really in your mind to come prowling back here, scaring me to distraction with that gray thing and the chinking and the horses and all?"

"The treasure," Perry said flatly. "There was no way that you were going to find it, fast as your sight was going. You needed doctoring then and you do now. I never had any use for that treasure of yours. I got all I wanted off of this place."

"And what might that be?" Boomer asked suspiciously.

"The only home I can ever remember," Perry said quietly. "A family who cared enough to take a rod to me when I needed it and buy me shoes for school and teach me to tie a fishing fly."

The long silence in the room was broken finally by the falling log in the fireplace.

Then Boomer spoke. "Well, Sheriff, I don't see that this boy has done anything to have charges pressed against him. That is, unless there's a charge about keeping an old man from making a fool of himself. And if there was such a charge, I wouldn't even bring that. I must owe him money, as a matter of fact. There's something called a 'finder's fee' where the fellow who finds hidden treasure gets to keep a part of it."

Then his expression grew crafty. "And like he said, we're family, him and me. He may be a hard-nosed pup who can't mind his own business but he might have learned a little of that from me, too. There don't have to be a charge, does there?"

"Not if you don't want to bring it." The sheriff grinned. He was trying to hide his amusement but there wasn't any reason for him to. The rest of us were all grinning, too, except Boomer, who couldn't see, and Perry, who seemed to be holding Boomer's words in his mind as if he meant to memorize them forever and ever.

After the sheriff had gone, Perry handed the items to Boomer one at a time out of the canvas bag. There were gold coins from some of the earliest mintings. There was a medal with a faded ribbon from the War of 1812. The thing I had felt with a spout on it was a teapot, and it had a sugar bowl and a bunch of plates to match.

"With that fortune in old silver and coins, you should never have to worry about money again," Mom said.

"The money isn't even the biggest thing," Boomer said quietly.

"Getting that treasure found must be a real thrill," I agreed, thinking of how long it had been since Emmaline fastened it down in the well.

"I didn't quite mean that either, Nathan," Boomer said, looking over toward Perry, who grinned at us a little red faced.

"Want me to wash up this coffee mess?"

Mom asked, rising to her feet. "The sheriff notified Dad that the kids and I were all right, but he's bound to watch the windows until we get in out of this storm."

"Leave them be," Perry said. "I've washed many a dish in that sink and I will again."

Perry saw us out to the car while Boomer stood waiting in the open door. Perry kept thanking us for all we had done. Mom was ready to start the engine when we heard a call and saw Boomer hanging onto the rope that was fastened to the trees and making his way toward us.

"So that's what that rope was for," I said without thinking.

Perry laughed. "I strung it up when his sight first started dimming. He really yelled at me but was using it within a week."

Boomer puffed a little from his haste. "I meant to ask you, Nan, did you ever find that compass?"

"No," Nan said, glancing at Mom and then quickly away.

"Compass?" Perry murmured. Then he groped under the poncho and pulled out Dad's genuine Army-Navy compass and held it out. "I found this one at the old house site early this week. Couldn't figure where it came from."

"Thank you, Perry," Mom said in a strange voice. She intercepted the compass before it reached Nan's hand. "I am sure that Nan thanks you, too," she said quietly.

There was an awkward silence as Mom drove toward home. Then suddenly she began to laugh. I decided she must be a little hysterical from the events of the afternoon because she kept laughing until the inside of the windshield was all clouded and there were tears streaming down her face.

When she finally got quieter, Nan spoke up in an injured tone. "I don't see anything funny."

"Give yourself time," Mom said gently, still with a little chuckle in her voice. "This has all been so scary and funny and *human*. That you could be such a perceptive and heroic little set of kids and still be such sneaks, like Boomer could be brave and proud while he lied to himself because he couldn't face the truth. And that Perry . . ." Her voice trailed off.

"Perry is something special," I agreed, thinking of his rough tone to Boomer even

126

while his eyes showed his love as clearly as Bubba's did.

"You all are," Mom said, bringing the car to a stop by the back door.

"Spoken like a true mother," I kidded her. I got out first because I wanted to open the door for Nan. Nobody else would notice that but she would know what I meant.

When she looked up at me I had a sudden terror that the little monster was going to say something sloppy or maybe even make fun of me. Instead she stuck out her tongue and caught a couple of snowflakes and then grinned at me.

"I love winter, don't you, Nathan?" she asked.

"It'll do," I agreed and swatted her on the behind as she flew past me toward the back door.

## ABOUT THE AUTHOR

MARY FRANCIS SHURA is the author of fifteen books for young people. Although she was born in Kansas, not far from Dodge City, the author has lived in many parts of the United States. Both of her parents came from early settler families of Missouri, where *The Gray Ghosts of Taylor Ridge* takes place. At least one incident from her own family history occurs in the book.

Aside from writing fiction for young readers and adults, Mary Francis Shura enjoys tennis, chess, reading, and cooking (especially making bread).

The author is married and the mother of a son, Dan, and three daughters, Minka, Ali, and Shay. She currently makes her home in the western suburbs of Chicago, in the village of Willowbrook.

## ABOUT THE ARTIST

MICHAEL HAMPSHIRE, illustrator of many children's books, grew up on Yorkshire's moors. An amateur archaeologist, he traveled extensively in Africa and the East before settling in New York City.